Erissa's

First Day of Kindergarten Jitters

ISBN 978-1-0980-6775-5 (paperback)
ISBN 978-1-0980-6776-2 (digital)

Christian Faith Publishing, Inc.
832 Park Avenue
Meadville, PA 16335
www.christianfaithpublishing.com

Printed in the United States of America

Erissa's First Day of Kindergarten Jitters

Lori McDonald

Erissa was very nervous the night before her first day of kindergarten. She could not fall asleep. All she could think about was the fun she had with her mom and little brother when she got to stay home. Erissa worried about what she might miss when she wasn't at home. Would Mommy be able to take care of her little brother, Asher? After Erissa finally fell asleep, she dreamed about her first day of school. Her dream was even more frightening than the thoughts she had when she was awake. Erissa dreamed about not having any friends. She dreamed about not knowing where the bathroom was. Erissa dreamed about getting lost and not finding her classroom. She dreamed about having disgusting snacks. She also dreamed about not knowing any correct answers.

Erissa's mom heard her crying and went into her room to see what was wrong. Erissa told her mom about her dream. Her mom assured her that everything would be fine. She even told Erissa that when she was a little girl, she had the same fears, but once she got to school, she loved it. None of her mommy's fears came true. After saying her prayers, getting up to use the restroom one more time, getting another drink of water, and choosing her fourth stuffed animal to keep her company, Erissa finally fell asleep.

Erissa woke up the next morning still feeling glum. She pretended to be sick. She told her mommy she wasn't hungry. She cried through breakfast. She even hid her shoes under her bed, trying to avoid having to get dressed. Once again, Erissa's mom talked to her and told her she would have fun at school. She reminded Erissa that Avery, her friend next door, would be at school and they could play together.

As they drove to school, Erissa continued to worry and think of all the bad things that could happen to her. She begged her mommy to let her stay at home with Asher so she could help take care of him. Erissa told her mommy that nobody could take care of her like her mommy could. She told her mommy that nobody would be at home to play with Asher. She said the teacher wouldn't love or care for her. Erissa even told her mom that none of the kids would be as much fun to play with as she was.

When they arrived at school, Erissa saw children playing outside. Some were playing soccer. Erissa was really good at soccer! Some kids were swinging. Erissa *loved* to swing and pretend she was flying. Erissa saw girls drawing with sidewalk chalk. She was a *great* artist. As Erissa and her mom walked to the classroom to hang up her backpack, Erissa saw her teacher. She had a very sweet smile and was holding a bunny. The teacher, Miss Sharp, introduced Erissa to the class pet, Fluffy. She asked Erissa if she would like to feed Fluffy some lettuce. When Erissa was busy feeding Fluffy, her mom quietly left.

The bell rang and all the children began rushing into the class. Miss Sharp greeted them all with a big smile. Erissa realized her mom had left, and all the worries and fears came rushing back. Miss Sharp told the students to find their name tag and have a seat at their table. Erissa found her name tag right next to her friend Avery's. She was so relieved to see a familiar face. Miss Sharp asked the children to write their names at the top of their papers. Erissa very slowly wrote her name, wanting to make sure she did it perfectly. Miss Sharp complimented her neat writing!

ERI

The children were asked to draw a picture of their families. Erissa drew beautifully and labeled each person. Miss Sharp commented how wonderful Erissa's picture was and told her she was a great artist. As the children lined up to tour the building, Erissa got to be the first one in line because her last name was Abraham and Miss Sharp had the children line up in ABC order. Being number one in line made Erissa feel very important. As they entered the room after touring the building, the students noticed the snack on their tables. Chocolate chip cookies and milk—Erissa's favorite! During "big circle," Miss Sharp led the students in reciting the Pledge of Allegiance to the United States flag. Suddenly, Erissa began to worry again because her mom had not taught her the words. She started to get a tummy ache. Erissa thought about her dream the night before and was afraid it was coming true. She wanted her mom. She wanted to go home and never go back to school.

Miss Sharp then played a game with the children. She asked them to tell her the beginning letter for the animal picture she held up. Erissa knew she would be great at this game because she already knew her letters and their sounds. Her mom had even taught her to read very easy words.

"P," they all shouted as Miss Sharp held up a picture of a pig.

"M," they announced when they saw a picture of a monkey.

"Z," the class stated for the baby zebra.

Erissa thought this was a very easy game. When the children saw the next picture, the room was silent. Some of the children guessed, but Miss Sharp kept saying, "No, try again."

Erissa finally came up with enough bravery to offer, "E."

Miss Sharp told Erissa she was correct. Erissa got to explain that she knew the picture was an emu because her grandparents had an emu farm. She was really excited that she was the only kid who knew the right answer! After the game, Miss Sharp told the students it was time to pack up their belongings because it was time to go home. Erissa couldn't believe how fast the morning went by. She was amazed that it was already time to go home.

PIG
ZEBRA
EMU

As the children waited for their parents, Miss Sharp asked them to find someone in the class who was like them. Some kids were grouped because they had the same color eyes or hair. Some were alike since they were wearing tennis shoes. A few girls were similar because they had on dresses. Finally, it was Miss Sharp's turn to find someone like her. She called Erissa's name because Miss Sharp's "real" name was Erissa, too! When Erissa's mom came to school to get her, Erissa didn't want to go home. She *loved* school and wanted to stay all day.

That night, when Erissa went to bed, she couldn't fall asleep. Her mommy heard her tossing and turning and went in to check on her. Erissa told her mom she wasn't having bad dreams; she was having great thoughts. Erissa told her mommy that when she grew up, she would be the best Kindergarten teacher *ever* (besides Miss Sharp)!

Anxiety: a feeling of worry, nervousness, or unease, typically about an imminent event or something with an uncertain outcome.

Worry: a state of anxiety and uncertainty over actual or potential problems; allow one's mind to dwell on difficulty or troubles.

Age-appropriate Bible verses to equip children with God's Holy Word.

"Trust in the Lord with all your heart" (Proverbs 3:5).

"The Lord bless you and keep you" (Numbers 5:24).

"I am with you always" (Matthew 28:20).

"When I am afraid, I will trust in you" (Psalm 56:3).

"I can do everything through Him who gives me strength" (Philippians 4:13).

Ideas for helping children overcome worry or anxiety:

Put a handwritten note in the child's lunchbox.

Draw a heart on the child's hand.

Send a photo of Mom and/or Dad in the child's backpack.

Allow the child to bring his/her favorite stuffed animal to leave in the backpack. Ask the teacher if the student could discretely look, touch, or smell the stuffed animal, if needed.

Reward the child with a sticker on a chart if the child is able to get up and get ready for school without tears. After earning a specified number of stickers, allow the child to choose the reward.

Draw a picture of the family to send in the child's backpack or lunchbox.

About the Author

Lori McDonald has been a public school teacher for twenty-five years. After teaching Early Childhood for twenty years, she went back to graduate school to get a master's degree in School Counseling. With mental health needing to be addressed in earlier years and in age-appropriate terms, Lori saw an opportunity to share her experiences to help children learn coping skills and how to talk to safe adults about issues that concern them. Lori believes that children's books are a wonderful, non-threatening way to show children that they are not alone when they experience various emotions. Books can allow readers to recognize and put into words the feelings and emotions they have experienced. Lori also saw writing this book as a way to equip parents, teachers, and caregivers with a few techniques that have proven beneficial to her in the classroom and as a counselor. This is the first book Lori McDonald has written. Lori grew up in Oklahoma City, Oklahoma, and still lives there with her husband of twenty-six years. They have two adult children.

CPSIA information can be obtained
at www.ICGtesting.com
Printed in the USA
BVHW021522250521
608098BV00009B/1945